Jer[illegible] Mastery

W.W. Rowe

LARSON PUBLICATIONS
BURDETT, NEW YORK

ISBN-10: 1-936012-80-4 | ISBN-13: 978-1-936012-80-0
eISBN-10: 1-936012-81-2 | eISBN-13: 978-1-936012-81-7

Library of Congress Control Number: 2016963556

Publisher's Cataloging-In-Publication Data
(Prepared by The Donohue Group, Inc.)
Names: Rowe, William Woodin.
Title: Jerry's mastery / W.W. Rowe.
Description: Burdett, New York : Larson Publications, [2017] | Series: [Jerry's M... series] ; [4] | Sequel to: Jerry's madness. | Interest age level: 010-013. | Summary: "[Jerry is] in the 8th grade. His relationship with Suzie is great, but his mom's not doing well. His cat Jade has died and his new puppy is acting strangely like her. He learns more about superstition, hypnosis, telepathy, karma, rebirth, and grace. He also learns the power of The Smile, and a new use of The Look."--Provided by publisher.
Identifiers: LCCN 2016963556 | ISBN 978-1-936012-80-0 | ISBN 1-936012-80-4 | ISBN 978-1-936012-81-7 (ebook) | 1-936012-81-2 (ebook)
Subjects: LCSH: Boys--Conduct of life--Juvenile fiction. | Sick parents--Juvenile fiction. | Pets--Juvenile fiction. | Telepathy--Juvenile fiction. | Reincarnation--Juvenile fiction. | CYAC: Boys--Conduct of life--Fiction. | Sick parents--Fiction. | Pets--Fiction. | Telepathy--Fiction. | Reincarnation--Fiction.
Classification: LCC PZ7.R7953 Jh 2017 (print) | LCC PZ7.R7953 (ebook) | DDC [Fic]--dc23

Published by Larson Publications
4936 NYS Route 414
Burdett, New York 14818 USA
https://www.larsonpublications.com

27 26 25 24 23 22 21 20 19 18 17
10 9 8 7 6 5 4 3 2 1

Front cover and interior illustrations: Benjamin Slatoff-Burke

Dedication

This book is gratefully dedicated to
Paul Brunton, Mark Twain, and
my wife Eleanor.

The goal is to free himself from meshes and fetters, to bring all the forces of his being under mastery.

—Paul Brunton

One who knows something of his past lives has something to throw light in some way on his present one.

—Paul Brunton

Pet animals do not end their existence at the body's end. Their invisible spirit form hovers around the vicinity of the master or mistress left behind.

—Paul Brunton

On Mastery

DID YOU EVER feel that the world was pointless, treacherous, and mean? That things were so bad, you didn't even care? Maybe you even *enjoyed* your suffering. You almost welcomed it . . . because it was all you could count on?

Poor you and your terrible, reliable suffering! You didn't deserve all those rotten potatoes, but you got them anyway. (Or could you have planted those very same potatoes sometime?)

Remember how you used to master things? When you cried in your crib and (presto change-o!) you were wearing a fresh diaper? Or when you giggled and threw your food, and your dish magically filled up again, and they said you were so adorable?

When did your life go off the tracks, anyway? And most important, what can you do now to master things again?

Mastery is hovering invisibly above your head like a Guardian Angel, hoping you'll learn how to find it, open your heart, and follow the intuition it provides. And maybe you will, after reading this book!

Disclaimer

IF YOU BOUGHT this book expecting to learn how to master the universe, don't bother suing. Who are you to order the planets and stars around, anyway? But if you're looking for a way to master Life, which can be a pretty mean critter, keep on reading. You might learn to turn your lemons into lemon meringue pie. Or even something amazingly better.

ONE

IT'S SPRING, and Jerry is thirteen now. Thirteen! Is it unlucky?

Peter Wardly thinks so. He's always been a little superstitious, but now he's almost kooky about it. He absolutely refuses to step on a crack in the sidewalk! When Willie Fielder playfully pushed him, so that one of Peter's big feet landed on a spidery crack, he actually screamed.

Jade the cat died last fall, on Jerry's thirteenth birthday. They were very close, so Jerry suffered plenty. His mother's desperate joke about a cat having nine lives didn't help much, either.

When Peter heard about Jade, he nodded solemnly. "See, Jerry? And that's only the beginning!" He shuddered. "All the guys are thirteen now. We'll be lucky to get through this year alive."

"Don't be an idiot," Cromer Borkin snarled. "You give me the creeps. Stop spouting that crazy stuff, or I'll give ya thirteen thumps for good luck."

Peter's eyes were blazing, so Jerry artfully switched the conversation to football.

Since then, the eighth grade has gone pretty smoothly. Except that Peter keeps doing more and more loony things. Like touching all the lockers in the hall when he gets to school. And wearing different colored socks. And making secret hand signs to keep disaster away.

What is it about thirteen? When Jerry was five, his father asked him: "What time is it when the clock strikes thirteen?" Little Jerry gave up. "Time to get the clock fixed," his papa said, and they both had a good laugh. But that was just silly.

Soon after that, Jerry's father went off to war and got killed. Jerry hasn't told Peter about the coincidence, which it surely was.

Last winter, a lot of kids got sick, especially Eva Ning. They'd get well, come back to school, and get sick again. There were rumors (maybe started by Peter) that they had some sort of mysterious disease, like scurvy, or jaundice, or even the plague. Eva is sick again now.

A bright spot has been provided by the "Doofus and Goofus" jokes that Willie Fielder tells. They're pretty stupid, but strangely enough, most of the guys can't wait to hear them.

Where does Willie get these jokes? From his Uncle Mort, who seems to be visiting his family forever. Here's the first one Willie told: "Doofus lies and says the dog ate his homework. So the teacher makes him take his dog to the vet and pay for it! Goofus is smarter. He says his homework was eaten by the neighbors' dog."

Most of the kids laughed at that, but some of them groaned.

Every day now, when Peter gets to class, he pulls from his pocket a little blue bag with a drawstring. Inside the bag are five good-luck charms: two large marbles painted like eyeballs, a green glass cat, a carved wooden basset hound, and a piece of rose quartz shaped like a pyramid.

Peter spreads the bag flat on his desk and places the charms carefully upon it, whispering an incantation. He sits there like a feverish Wizard, casting urgent spells.

When Monty Flowers remarked that it hasn't really been an unlucky year, Peter grabbed him by the shoulders. "Don't you get it?" he said, his voice choking with emotion. "These charms keep disaster away!"

Five kids were sick today, so there were only a dozen in English class. The teacher, Mr. Stim, made thirteen, so Peter excused himself and went to the washroom, where he lingered for the whole period.

This is getting serious, Jerry thinks. But thirteen isn't always bad. His father once explained that thirteen is "a baker's dozen." If you bought a dozen cookies, say, or a dozen corn muffins, the baker might add an extra one. It was good business. So thirteen could be good luck too, couldn't it?

After school, Jerry walks Suzie home, carrying her books atop his own. She skips lightly along on the sidewalk. It's a warm, breezy afternoon. Her dark-blue eyes sparkle, and her blonde curls bounce.

"Aren't all those books too heavy?"

"For you, fair maiden, I'd tote an entire library on my back."

"Jer-ee! You're so sweet." Suzie flutters her eyelids . . . and his heart makes a wild leap.

They walk in blissful silence for a while.

Suzie twists her face into a puzzled frown. "I feel sorry for Peter. He's acting weirder and weirder."

"Yeah, he's got thirteen-itis."

"What?"

"You know. We're all thirteen now, and that's unlucky. Peter is afraid that a giant hairy hand will swoop down from the clouds and squeeze us like helpless lemons."

Suzie giggles nervously. "It's not a joke, is it? He really believes we're doomed, doesn't he?"

"Well, yeah. But he thinks maybe he can prevent

it. If he touches lockers and mumbles to the charms on his desk."

"Molly says he's going to a psychiatrist."

"I don't think so. I'd have heard. But if he keeps getting worse . . ." Jerry's words fade away like little birds, flapping toward the horizon.

"I'm glad you're normal, Jerry." She gives him a zingy look from the corner of her eyes.

Jerry smiles. "Sure. Except for my bottle of whispering beans. When I get home, I hold them up beside my ears."

"Jer-ee!" Suzie laughs, pushing him on the shoulder. "Give me those books. We just passed my house."

Jerry completely forgets about Peter. Suzie haunts him—like an Angel who floated down from her celestial palace to caper on the Earth. He walks mechanically, his thoughts weaving pleasant daydreams.

Before he knows it, he's home. Above the house, a golden cloud reclines like a lazy lion, or maybe a cat. It makes Jerry think of Jade, and he shudders. As he goes up the front walk, the cloud looks more like a dog. *The wind must be blowing hard up there.*

He barges in the front door, slinging his books on the floor. Then he hesitates, cocks his head. Something seems different.

Jerry hears a sliding scrape. A muffled thump. A strange yelp. Coming from the kitchen.

For one horrible moment, he pictures his mother tied to a kitchen chair, struggling with a gag in her mouth.

"Mom!"

Jerry dashes into the kitchen and comes up short, staring with wide, bulging eyes.

TWO

"MOM! What the—"

"Jerry! Watch where you step."

His mother is bending down, covering the kitchen floor with newspapers.

A clumsy puppy lumbers over. He wags his tail and licks Jerry's hand.

"He's a pure-bred basset hound." Jerry's mother smiles. "And his name is Lohengrin."

"What?" Jerry already has the puppy in his arms. A big wet tongue slurps across his cheek. He flashes on a book his dad used to read to him when he was little: *Howard the Happy Basset Hound.*

"Low and grin, get it? Your father always wanted to call a dog that. Maybe it will get his attention even better than the mushroom soup."

"Yeah, maybe it will." Jerry frowns, thinking of Sister Sorsy, who suggested making his father's favorite soup to attract his spirit. "How do you know Dad hasn't been reborn by now?"

"Mercy! Wilcox told you about rebirth, didn't he? Well, I just sense that your father is sticking around . . . to see what you and I are doing." She sniffles softly. "He was killed so suddenly in the War, bravely rushing straight ahead, and then that awful mistake from behind. He wrote me before that he would surely come home, and your father was a very determined man."

"You've told me that already."

"Well, it's true. Anyway, I couldn't resist Lowey. He already answers to that. He's so smart! I was walking past Percy's Pets, and he kept jumping up against the window. It was almost spooky, like he was picking *me* out. Look at those eyes!"

"He's, uh, very cute, Mom." *But he'll never replace Jade.*

Lowey yips excitedly, like he can read Jerry's mind.

"There's something funny about his bark, Mom. It's sort of squeaky."

"Well, he's just a puppy. He'll develop a more mature voice later. He'll grow into those funny folds of skin too. But look at his intelligent eyes!" She grabs onto a chair. "Ooh!"

"What's the matter, Mom?"

"Just a little dizzy spell. I'm all right now. I don't even need a pill."

Jerry watches her carefully. She's been having these dizzy spells a lot recently. Dr. Trainer gives her pills for vertigo, and they seem to help.

Supper is mac and cheese, which used to be Jerry's favorite. He doesn't want to disappoint his mother, so he makes a big fuss.

"This is really great, Mom! Good old mac n' cheese."

"Glad you like it. Have another helping."

"I've had two already."

"You usually have three." She stretches her neck. "Look how Lowey's eating. Puppies are natural magicians. They transform food into poop before you can even turn around! He favors the corner where Jade's litter box used to be. I cleaned the floor there carefully too. But dogs can smell a million times better than people."

"Uh, I think that's a thousand times, Mom."

"Maybe. But he's still scary smart. "See? He's finished his food already."

Lohengrin lurches over and whines.

"No, Lowey. You had yours." Jerry's mother throws a red rubber bone, but the puppy ignores it.

"He smells the mac and cheese, Mom."

"Well, he'll just have to learn. How was school today?"

Jerry stops buttering a roll. "The usual. But Peter's getting more and more superstitious. He has to touch the lockers on *both* sides of the hall now."

"Mercy! Your father used to say that superstition is a pacifier for childish minds. But that boy seems headed for trouble."

"Some kids say Peter is going to a psychiatrist already. He thinks he's saving us from disaster, 'cause we're all thirteen." Jerry thoughtfully licks the end of his fork. "Psychological problems aren't contagious, are they?"

His mother laughs. "Heavens, I hope not! We'd all be lined up for the loony bin."

Jerry shrugs. "Some kids are still out sick. I heard that Eva has a really serious illness."

Jerry's mother nods. "I'm sorry. Stop that, Lowey. Stop!"

In a far corner of the kitchen, the puppy is snorting and hissing. He's shaking his blanket in his jaws, like it's alive and trying to escape. But when he hears the word *stop*, he actually does.

"Look at that, Jerry! I told you he was smart. I wonder what got into him."

Before bed, Jerry takes Lowey out to the backyard, where he immediately poops and pees between the rose bushes.

"Good boy!" Jerry runs him around the big pine

several times so he'll be nice and tired. Maybe he'll sleep all night.

Up in his room, Jerry wonders what he can do to help Peter. He pictures his earnest, rat-like face. Peter has always been pretty intense. He grinds his teeth a lot. Three years ago, he got all excited about Jerry's Bad-Dream Protector. Last year, he absolutely had to have Fox's sexy flip book (before Fox broke his leg and went back to France). And now, Peter's convinced that "thirteen" spells doom for the entire eighth grade.

Just last week, Peter told everyone about a dream he had. The world was coming to an end, with fires everywhere, and a new ice age too. But Peter, in the dream, discovered a way to save the human race! Only now he can't remember what it was. His charms are the next best thing, at least until he can think of what his dream-self did to fend off disaster.

Peter said he woke up with his blanket around his head and his legs bare. Willie said: "No wonder. That explains the fire and ice in the dream. Your feet were cold, and your head was hot."

Peter laughed bitterly. "Hardly, my friend," he declared, slowly grinding his teeth.

Jerry said the dream was probably triggered by the poem they read in Mr. Stim's class, "Fire and Ice" by Robert Frost. The world was supposed to end in one or the other.

Peter liked that explanation even less. "How can

you ignore the evidence?" he growled. "It was clearly a prophetic dream!"

Willie smirked. "Don't forget the name Frost," he said, stifling a laugh. "That's where the ice came from."

Cromer Borkin laughed. "Your next dream will be about cake frosting."

"Monday, fun day," Peter snarled. "Tuesday, dues day!" He stormed away, furious.

Now, up in his bedroom, Jerry sighs. He meditates for a while, thinking of his Higher Self. He prays for a way to help Peter come to his senses. He prays for his mother's dizziness to stop.

THREE

IT'S MORNING. Pajama-clad, Jerry yawns at his window. The clouds look murky and swirly, like there's a ghostly free-for-all up in the sky.

In the kitchen, his mother greets him with a delighted smile. "Lowey didn't poop or pee all night! I told you he was smart. And when I took him out, he went both ways."

Jerry's already down on the floor, getting his face licked. "He's really friendly, Mom. But his bark is still squeaky."

"We've got to be careful not to spoil him." She gives Jerry a meaningful look. "He's already had his breakfast."

Jerry nods. Soon he's plowing through a huge plate of pancakes and sausage.

Lowey almost sits up, flopping clumsily down.

"Did you see that, Mom? He's teaching himself! Can I give him some sausage?"

"Well, I guess so. One little piece. Mercy! He'll be spoiled before the week is out." She looks out the kitchen window. "Be sure to wear your raincoat today."

In his chair, Jerry raises up from giving Lowey two large hunks of sausage. "Right, Mom."

He shudders. His mother is taking a pill for dizziness. She's trying to slip it down secretly, but he sees.

"Uh, Mom, don't you think maybe you should see a specialist?"

"What? Oh, you mean for these pesky dizzy spells. I'm doing just fine with Dr. Trainer's pills, thank you. Your father used to say that specialists are like lawyers, except that specialists rob you blind and kill you as well." She laughs weakly. "He got that from the Russian writer Chekhov . . . who was also a doctor, by the way, so he knew."

At school, Willie begins the day with a new joke. "What trick does Doofus use to get a date?" he asks in a loud voice.

All the guys crowd around, listening closely. Even the girls. Especially the girls.

Willie grins. "Doofus waits just outside the movie theater. If a girl is going to the movies anyway, it's harder for her to say no. Goofus is smarter. He waits just inside the theater, so he doesn't have to pay for the girl's ticket."

Most of the guys laugh, but Peter has a strained look on his face. He announces that he's holding off a terrible flood with charms, hand signs, and incantations.

"Sure is working!" Willie smirks. He lets out a short snicker.

"Go ahead," says Peter. "Have your fun. But you'll thank me when the flood doesn't come."

Willie rolls his eyes. "Oh, yeah. I'll be eternally grateful."

After school, despite the ominously darkening clouds, Jerry heads for the junkyard, where his friend and mentor Wilcox lives in a slapdash cardboard house.

Wilcox knows the answers to just about everything Jerry cares about. He and Jerry sometimes do telepathy together. Now, tramping through the forest, Jerry sends the thought that he needs to talk.

Jerry! Come on over. Haven't seen you for a while.

Thanks. I'll be there soon.

Wilcox is sitting cross-legged in front of his fragile house, as usual. His face is peaceful, seemingly oblivious to the gathering storm. He's wearing his faded red headband and a thick brown sweater.

Jerry sits down beside the old man. "Nice sweater."

Wilcox opens his eyes. "Thank you. Somebody

dumped a box of old clothes, right over there. I only had to sew up the shoulder." He stretches and smiles. "What brings you here this fine gloomy day?"

Jerry looks vaguely at the mass of dark clouds, as if Peter's condition is written on them in bold, bright letters. "It's Peter Wardly. He's getting more and more superstitious." Jerry watches the clouds swirl and churn. "He's doing really weird things. They aren't even funny anymore."

Wilcox looks concerned. "There are two kinds of superstitions, you know. One is like an All-Day Sucker. The other, Ambrosia."

Jerry smiles faintly. He knows that an All-Day Sucker is a giant lollipop, and he appreciates the pun. But what is Ambrosia? He doesn't want to seem dumb, so he'll look it up later, in the dictionary.

Wilcox continues. "One is everyday silliness. You spill the salt and throw some over your shoulder. It's harmless, unless your belief gets out of control." He turns serious. "But once in a great while, it's possible to get in tune with your Higher Self. At such a time, you may be able to sense a hint of what is to come, a tiny insight into Nature's Grand Design."

Jerry gulps. "Nature's what?"

"Grand Design. The universe has a karmic pattern of destiny. Some say that when we are born, even our probable place and time of death are already established."

Jerry gapes. "Sounds like we're ants, waiting to be crushed. Or little wind-up toys."

Wilcox laughs. "Oh, we have plenty of free will in our waking dream. Don't worry about that. We can choose, for example, to believe in outlandish superstitions. Tell me more about Peter."

"Well, he was late to school one day because a black cat crossed his path. He made a big detour, so he could approach from the other direction. He always wears different colored socks now. And he has to touch the lockers on both sides of the hall at school. He's even started touching some of the other kids. On the top of their heads."

Wilcox's eyes widen. "What does he say?"

"That we're all thirteen now, and he's keeping disaster away."

"Ah, teens. The treacherous doorway to adulthood."

Jerry frowns. "But thirteen isn't really unlucky, is it?"

"Not unless you rob thirteen banks." Wilcox grins. "You're not planning to do that, are you?"

Jerry laughs. "You know I'm not."

"Well then, no worries. We make our own luck, which is the result of what we think and do, in this life or a previous one." The grin is now a kindly smile.

"I've been praying for Peter at night, but it doesn't seem to help."

Wilcox nods. "You can never tell when a prayer will be answered." He looks at Jerry carefully. "There's something else, isn't there?"

Jerry gapes. How does Wilcox know? "Well, yeah. I'm worried about my mom. Her dizzy spells are getting worse. She takes pills for them."

Wilcox nods gravely. "Please keep me informed."

"Sure." Jerry sighs. "But right now, I'm more worried about Peter. I'm afraid he'll get into serious trouble. I've, uh, been thinking of using The Look to help him. Would that be okay?"

Wilcox grabs Jerry's arm. "Probably not. As you know, The Look is sometimes necessary to prevent something very bad from happening. But if hypnotism is used for healing, it can weaken a person, possibly even make him worse."

"Even if *you* do it? I think Peter's in real danger."

Wilcox thinks for a minute. "I don't like to impose my will on someone else unless it's absolutely necessary. If I helped Peter to *cheat his bad karma,* it would hit him anyway, in some other form. He'd soon be in some other kind of trouble. We all must do things for ourselves."

Jerry gives him a pleading look. "I understand. But Peter's problems just seem to get worse. Isn't there something you can do?"

Wilcox stares into space. His eyes glaze over. Soon he's in one of his trances.

Jerry waits hopefully.

Wilcox sits quietly.

Soon he speaks in a slightly different voice. "Old karma from the distant past . . . can ripen strangely, very fast."

He's still in the trance. Jerry waits patiently.

After a few more minutes, Wilcox snaps his head. "Perhaps I can use The Look as a bridge to locate the cause of Peter's problem."

"Cool!"

"My teacher said I have a rare aptitude for this. But it's not a game, Jerry. We must remember that silly as Peter's fears may seem, he really believes them. Can you bring him here?"

Jerry jumps up. "Sure! I mean, I think so. What should I tell him?"

"You'll have to figure that out for yourself. Just let me know when you're ready."

"I'll do it. Even if I have to tie him up with magic rope." Jerry laughs. "Thanks, Wilcox!"

FOUR

THE NEXT day, rain falls relentlessly. It's "roaring pain," as Jerry's father used to say, whereupon little Jerry would giggle at the spoonerism. Now, he walks Lowey in the water-saturated backyard. The puppy seems afraid of the puddles. He strains on the leash to go back.

Snatching up the willful dog, Jerry sloshes over to the big pine. On the carpet of matted needles beneath its branches, Lowey performs creditably well. Still, they get soaked, and Jerry dries the puppy with old towels.

In school, Suzie says it's raining cats and dogs, and Jerry twitches.

Peter is gloomier than ever. "I knew it," he tells everyone. "But I'm doing a rain-chasing spell to make it stop."

Just before supper, Lowey and Jerry are playing on the floor of his room when the puppy utters a screechy noise. It sounds eerily like one of Jade's meows. Jerry flashes back on what happened a few months ago . . .

Jade had stopped eating—even her favorite sardines. She made low, soft moans. She seemed sleepy and limp. Her green eyes weakly glowed.

After a while Jerry's mother declared: "It's time for the vet."

She drove while Jerry held Jade. The cat trembled and whined.

After a long series of tests, Dr. Kurr sighed. It's cancer, he said, twirling his thin mustache. "There's a lot of internal bleeding. I'm afraid we need to put Jade down."

With a jolt, Jerry realized what this meant. After waiting so long, he only had time for a couple of hugs and one gentle kiss.

Now, as he lies on the floor, tears run down his face. Lowey stops playing. The puppy whimpers and cuddles up close, like he understands. Jerry hugs him, thinking of Jade.

It rains steadily for two whole days.

At school, the kids stand in the hall, peeling off their dripping rain-gear. The guys make jokes about how to save the human race from a terrible flood. They plan to build a giant ark with bedrooms for their girlfriends.

Molly Kewel says the human race doesn't need saving *that* much.

Willie blurts out one of his so called jokes. "How does Doofus tell if it's raining? He holds his hand out *inside* the house. Goofus is smarter. He holds out *his* hand up in the attic."

Most of the kids reluctantly laugh.

But not Peter. His long rat-face is shrouded with gloom. He stalks some of the other guys now, tapping their foreheads three times to hex the evil spirits causing the rain.

Whoa! Jerry thinks. *This is getting really weird.*

He walks up to Peter in the hallway. "The rain will stop soon, you know. It always does."

"Don't be so sure." Peter makes a frustrated sigh. "My mom, she . . ." He grips Jerry's arm so hard it hurts. "She opened her umbrella *inside* the house yesterday, before she went out." His face goes pale as a ghost. "And this morning, there was a foot of water in our basement."

Jerry shrugs. "There's been a record amount of rain. I heard about it on the radio."

"And why do you think so much came?" Peter glares at Jerry scornfully. "I'll tell you another thing." He lowers his voice. "My mom killed a spider . . . and she wouldn't say *Bite Be Gone*—even when I begged her."

"Bite be gone?"

"Yes. Bite doesn't mean a spider bite, of course. It stands for misfortune or calamity."

Jerry stares. "Where do you, uh, get these ideas, Peter?"

"Everybody knows some of 'em." Peter leans closer. "But I've got this special book." He whispers confidentially. "It's called *Dreams, Omens, and Portents: How to Ward off Disaster.* I found it at Barnaby's Book Shop. The old guy practically gave it away."

"*Ward* off? That's a good one!"

Jerry stops smiling when Peter doesn't. "I was just thinking of your last name. How do you know these things are true?"

"They *work,* Jerry. Every one I've tested. The proof is in the pudding! Sometimes my fingers tingle too, like when I do rain-chasing spells."

Jerry shrugs. What can he say?

Peter grinds his teeth. "I could have told you Jade would die. The morning of your thirteenth birthday, I saw a face on my toast. A cat's ears and eyes. Even a few whiskers. And a toast face portends death."

Jerry gapes in surprise. "Did you save it?"

"Yes. I put it on a napkin, and told my mom. But my dad didn't hear, and he ate it." Peter scowls. "Eating a bad omen brings even worse luck."

"Is that what your book says?"

"Of course." Peter points out the window. "See

those drifting rain clouds?" He smiles grimly. "They're shaped like coffins."

Jerry nods uncertainly. "Well, I wouldn't say . . ."

"They clearly signify death, but who will it be?" Peter solemnly scratches his head. And how will it happen? That's the question. A random shooting? A stealthy poison? A gruesome car accident?"

Jerry half suspects that Peter is pulling his leg. If he fails to laugh, Peter might make fun of him, tell the whole class. But if Peter is sincere, he'd better buy into it.

All this rushes through Jerry's mind in a couple of seconds. He needs to act right away, to make it seem natural. He smacks his head, as if he's suddenly remembered something.

"Hey, Peter, I've got a friend who can help us figure it out."

"Who?" Peter leans closer. "What friend?"

"His name is Wilcox."

"That crazy old loon who lives at the dump? The guy they call Crazy Wilcox?"

Jerry tries not to be offended. "He's an expert on omens and portents."

Peter stares. "Are you sure?"

Jerry nods seriously. "He's predicted a lot of things for me. And they've all come true."

Peter narrows his eyes. "Such as?"

Uh-oh. Jerry thinks fast. "Well, yesterday he said I

would bring someone whose name . . . begins with P to see him tomorrow. On Saturday morning."

Peter's eyes go wide. His jaw trembles. "That . . . that explains the penny I found this morning. Finding a penny means a new friend."

Jerry smiles. "What did I tell you? I'll come by your house tomorrow at ten."

"Even in the rain?"

"Even if it's raining lions and tigers."

When Jerry gets home, he walks Lowey. The puppy shies away from the puddles, but he does his business under the big pine.

"Good boy!" Jerry dries him off in the kitchen. Then he races up to his room. It's time for some urgent telepathy.

Wilcox! Wilcox! Do you read me?

Loud and clear. What is it?

I, uh, persuaded Peter to come and see you. Tomorrow morning. Is that okay?

Sure.

I, uh, told him you're an expert on omens and portents.

That was bending the truth.

Sorry. Will you still see him?

Yes.

FIVE

SATURDAY dawns bright and clear. Jerry smiles grimly. Peter's rain-chasing spells finally worked.

Springing out of bed, he gazes out the window. High in the blue sky, snowy cloud-wisps are racing by. One is triangular, shaped like a pyramid.

Throwing on some clothes, Jerry runs down and hugs Lowey on the kitchen floor. The puppy wriggles and whines with pleasure.

Breakfast is French toast and bacon, but Jerry hardly notices. He's too busy anticipating what Wilcox will do with Peter.

Jerry's mother secretly takes a pill. "A penny for your thoughts, dear."

A penny! Jerry wipes maple syrup from his bulging

cheeks. "I was, uh, thinking about Peter, Mom." He slips Lowey a whole strip of bacon.

"Oh, that poor misguided boy."

"I'm planning to take him to see Wilcox."

"Really? That's wonderful! He can help if anyone can."

"Yeah. Peter has started running out into the street to touch slowly moving cars." Another strip of bacon disappears.

"Heavens to Betsy! Why does he do that?" She squints over her glasses. "And don't spoil that dog."

Jerry nods. He takes a long drink of milk. "Peter is still trying to save us from doom. He calls it *draining danger away*."

"Mercy! Does Wilcox think he can help?"

"It's complicated. He'll try, but he hasn't promised results."

Jerry wears the mysterious expression that tells his mother there's no point in asking any more questions.

"Well, I hope he can do something. If Peter runs out to touch moving cars, it's not just dangerous for him, but for someone else . . . if the car swerves to miss him."

Just before ten, Jerry pounds on Peter's door. It opens after only two thumps. "Hi, Jerry. My rain-chasing spells finally worked!" He smiles. "But draining danger away is tiring. I hope your friend can help."

So do I. Jerry nods. "Well, like I said, he's an expert on omens and portents."

Peter's eyes narrow. "Good. He'd better be!"

Jerry smiles. "He'll do something amazing to help us avoid disaster. You'll see."

They walk through the woods in silence. A lone bird chirps in a tall oak tree.

Jerry concentrates his mind. *Hi, Wilcox. We're on the way.*

Peter turns to Jerry. "How do you know he'll be there?"

Good. Did you need to use magic rope?

No. It was easy. But he's suspicious. I told him you'd do something amazing to help him avoid disaster.

Peter raises his voice. "Jerry! Did you hear me? How do you know he'll be there?"

"Whuh? Oh, I just know. Don't worry."

"But what will he do that's so amazing?"

"You'll see. We're almost there."

When I put him under, you must be very quiet, no matter what he says. All right?

Sure.

"What's wrong with you, Jerry?"

"Huh? Whuh?"

"You looked like you were hypnotized or something. Ha ha."

Jerry laughs too. "Oh, I was just wondering what

you'll think of what Wilcox does. It'll be amazingly amazing!"

Wilcox sits cross-legged, as usual, before his cardboard house. "Hi, Jerry. I see you've brought a friend."

"Wilcox, this is Peter. Peter, Wilcox."

Wilcox stands up, holds out his hand. "A pleasure, Peter."

"Nice to meet you, Mr. Wilcox."

"At least the rain has stopped." Wilcox offers them pieces of dry cardboard. Please sit down."

They sit, forming a tight triangle. Wilcox looks into Peter's eyes.

Peter twitches with excitement. "Jerry says you can do amazing things. And I need help with—"

Peter's head slumps limply forward. Wilcox has him under already!

"Now, Peter. I want you to relax completely, but hold your head up. Can you hear me?"

"Yes." Peter's head rises back up. "I hear you."

"Good. Feel your body relax. You're going deep into the past.

"Waah."

"Even before that, Peter. Long before you were a baby in this life. Way, way back."

Peter squirms, wiggles, smiles.

"Good. Who are you now?"

"My name is Fanny Lang. I'm on the platform,

pulling off my clothes. All the drunks are leering, and my legs are cold." He shivers slightly.

Jerry's eyes grow wide. Peter was a stripper! In this life, he wanted Fox's sexy flipping pad so much. There might be a connection . . .

"That's all right," says Wilcox. "But you need to go even further back. Back to yet another life."

Peter raises his arm. His fingers close, like he's holding something.

"What is that in your hand?"

"My, uh, net."

"Who are you now?"

Peter hesitates. I'm a rat-catcher, I think. My name is Ezra. Ezra Kreese."

Jerry smiles. *Rat-faced Peter was a rat-catcher!*

"That's all right. Now you must go even further into the past. *Way* back."

Peter nods. He starts stroking his hair, like he's grooming himself. "I am Zarah, Queen of Egypt."

Jerry's mouth falls wide open. *Peter was . . . a queen!* He's about to say something, but Wilcox waves his arm, puts a finger to his lips.

"What are you doing now?"

Peter frowns. "My Chief Seer, Cholat, has warned me again . . . about a rebellion in my army. He wants to hold a protection ceremony, with purifying fires, charms, and incantations. But that is unnecessary. My army is loyal!" Peter smiles dreamily. "Cholat is wonderfully handsome. But he snores."

Wilcox looks serious. "What is happening now, Queen Zarah?"

Peter grows angry. "I'm refusing to hold the ceremony. I'm scoffing at Cholat's spells and charms." Suddenly, he shakes his head. He begins to sob. "The uprising has occurred! So many of my people are killed! I should have allowed Cholat to prevent this disaster."

Wilcox gently grips Peter's arm. "It's all right. What is happening now?"

"Now I'm being thrown into prison. The traitor Forvus is King."

Jerry gapes.

Wilcox nods. "I think we have solved your problem, Queen Zarah. Now listen carefully. Cholat's charms would *never* have been effective. The rebellion had been brewing for a long time. It would have happened anyway. So there is no need to feel guilty."

"No need . . . to feel guilty."

"Yes. You will now go forward in time until you are Peter again."

"Peter again."

"Good. When you open your eyes, you will not be superstitious. You will know that superstitions are silly. Very silly. You will know that something amazing just happened, but you won't remember what."

"Won't remember what."

"Right. When you wake up, the number thirteen will be just like any other. There will be no need for charms of any kind. When I count to three, you will open your eyes."

"Open my eyes."

"Yes. And you will be a calm, unworried Peter. One, two, three."

Walking back through the woods, Jerry claps Peter on the back. "Wasn't that amazing?"

"Huh? Oh, yeah." He closes his eyes, like he's trying to remember. "It really . . . was. Yes!"

"How do you feel, Peter?"

"What do you mean? I feel just like before."

Uh-oh. Jerry's heart falls. "But we're thirteen now. Do we need to worry about that?"

Tipping his head back, Peter brays like a donkey. "Don't be ridiculous! It's silly to be superstitious. I'm surprised at you, Jerry."

Whew! Jerry heaves an inner sigh of relief. "Yeah, I guess you're right, Peter."

SIX

WHEN Jerry gets home, his mother and Lowey are waiting on the front porch. She's in her rocker and the puppy is lying at her feet, playing with a ball of purple yarn.

"Mom! It worked! Wilcox cured Peter!"

"Rayowrl!" Lowey barks, but it sounds weird.

"That's wonderful, dear. I have some exciting news too."

"Peter is totally cured! He's not superstitious anymore." Jerry jumps up onto the porch. "The world has stopped coming to an end."

Lowey growls, rolling the ball of yarn with his paw.

"I'm so glad, Jerry." She rises to her feet, but suddenly sits back down, holding her head. "I talked with Sister Sorsy this morning, and you won't believe what she told me.

I probably won't. "What, Mom?"

"You know how Lowey's bark has been so strange?"

"Yeah, sure." Jerry yawns.

"And how he *went* in the corner where Jade's litter box used to be?"

"Sure, Mom. So what?"

"Brace yourself, dear." She makes a smug smile. "Lowey is haunted! Sister Sorsy saw it in her crystal ball."

Jerry's mouth falls open. Sister Sorsy has said some kooky things about his father's ghost, but this is too much! "When did Dad, uh, do this?"

"Not your father, dummy. Sister Sorsy assured me that his spirit still watches us." She takes a deep breath. "It's Jade! Don't you see? After Jade passed away, her spirit hovered near me, wanting to communicate. When I approached the pet store, she saw an opportunity. Jade decided to use Lowey as an agent. Quick as a flash, her spirit entered him. Remember how I said the puppy chose *me*?"

Jerry's mind is in a whirl. This is totally crazy! But it might explain some strange things, like the puppy's fear of water in the yard. He looks down. Lowey is toying with the ball of yarn in a definitely catlike way. "I, uh, I dunno, Mom. This is pretty weird."

"Of course it is, dear. At first, I couldn't believe it either. But I remember feeling funny little tingles on the sidewalk. That was Jade's presence, floating beside me. And when Sister Sorsy saw the struggle in her crystal ball, I began to understand—"

"What struggle?"

"Between the dog's body and the cat's spirit. That's why he makes those strange sounds. He's trying to bark, but Jade makes it sound more like a cat."

Jerry squats down beside Lowey. Holding the puppy's head, he looks deeply into his eyes. "Jade! Are you . . . in there?"

Lowey makes a strange little whimper.

"He can't tell you, of course. But Sister Sorsy is *positive*."

Jerry looks up. "You know what the kids say about her, Mom. She's the world's number one kook. Hey, wait! How, did you, uh, happen to talk with Sister Sorsy?"

"She called me up. Can you believe it? She said she'd been thinking about me, so she consulted her crystal ball. That's what she said, *consulted*, and there I was, walking along the sidewalk."

"So? Lots of people walk on sidewalks."

"Yes, but she actually *saw* me in the ball. And when I told her about Percy's Pets, she said that's exactly where it was."

Oh, so you told her first. Jerry smiles knowingly. "Hey! Did you tell her Jade died—and that Lowey was acting like a cat?"

"Jerry, if you're going to have a closed mind, we

won't be able to discuss this intelligently."

"Sorry, Mom." Jerry tries not to roll his eyes.

"That's all right. I understand how strange it seems. But Sister Sorsy even saw Jade's spirit enter the puppy! So there, Mr. Smarty Pants." She makes a satisfied smile. "And that's not all. I gave Lowey a saucer of milk. He lapped it up and purred exactly like Jade!"

Jerry narrows his eyes. "Purred?"

"Well, it certainly wasn't a doggie noise. He even hounded me for more. Hey, that's funny, isn't it? Hounded. And look how he's playing with that ball of yarn. Cats could take lessons!"

Jerry's head is spinning. He doesn't know what to think. First, Peter was a Queen of Egypt. And now, Jade is haunting Lowey! What's next? A spaceship full of little green men with shiny black eyes?

He shakes his head. "What's for lunch, Mom?"

"Tuna sandwiches, of course. We're going to celebrate Jade's return."

They munch in silence at the kitchen table. Lowey sits excitedly in Jerry's mother's lap. "See? He absolutely loves tuna! If that doesn't convince you, I give up."

Lowey's tongue is busy slurping her fingertips.

"Any dog will eat tuna fish, Mom."

"Not with such . . . delicate enthusiasm. He dines exactly like Jade, licking around his mouth after he swallows."

Jerry helplessly shrugs his shoulders. "Sister Sorsy strikes again," he mutters.

That afternoon, Jerry takes Lowey up to his room. The puppy lies on the rug, licking one paw and using it to wipe the side of his face.

Jerry stares and stares. "Jade!" he whispers. "Jade?"

Lowey stretches and whines.

Supper is a strange event. Jerry is thinking about Peter's amazing cure. His mother still tingles with the news of Jade's haunting influence. And they're both watching Lowey from the corners of their eyes.

"Good pot roast, Mom."

"Thanks. Remember how I used to call it rot post? You used to giggle at that." She grimaces and takes a pill.

"Uh, yeah, I remember."

Having wolfed down his dinner, Lowey stretches. He makes a yawning, screechy sound.

Jerry and his mother both jump.

"Hear that, Jerry? Jade is definitely inside him! How can we let her know that *we* know?"

"I dunno, Mom. I'd feel weird calling Lowey Jade."

"So would I." She clatters down her teacup with a trembling hand. "Maybe she *knows* we know, anyway. But does Lowey know he's haunted? He probably doesn't understand what's happening."

Jerry watches the puppy stretch. "He, uh, seems to be fighting the cat influence, Mom. He doesn't want to act that way, but he can't resist."

"You're right, Jerry. He looks uncomfortable now."

"Maybe we should take him to the vet, Mom. For help with his, uh, split personality."

"Mercy! What would we say to Dr. Kurr? He'd get *us* locked up in the loony bin!"

Lowey is sitting up now, dangling his paws. He manages to look cute.

"Look at that, Jerry. His dog nature is asserting itself. I've got to reward that." She holds out a chunk of meat."

Jerry feeds Lowey a piece of meat too.

"Heavens! He'll soon weigh a hundred pounds. But look how daintily he took it! No doggie ever had manners like that. "He must have a constant battle going on inside."

"Wilcox might know what to do," says Jerry.

"Maybe you're right." His mother shrugs. "But I trust Sister Sorsy. I'm going to give her a call."

SEVEN

IT'S SUNDAY morning. Jerry's mother fixes sausages and creamy oatmeal with raisins. Jerry notices that her hands are shaking. Lowey is prowling around the stove, eagerly sniffing the air.

"Is everything okay, Mom?"

"Yes, dear." She takes a quick sip of tea, washing down a pill. "It's just that I had the strangest dream. I was standing here in the kitchen with Lowey, and he could talk!"

Jerry smiles. "What did he say?"

"*Hi there*. Just two words, but I almost dropped the bowl of strawberries I was holding." Her eyes are huge, remembering. "Then I gasped: *You can talk!* And Lowey said: *Haunted dogs always talk*. And I said, *Oh*. I mean, what else could I say?"

Jerry laughs. "What happened after that?"

"He looked at me severely and said: *If you don't get that bossy cat out of my head, I'm going back to Percy's Pets*. Imagine!" She rattles down her teacup. "And that's not all. A whiny, high-pitched voice said: *Don't listen to that stupid hound. I'm in charge here!* Then the two voices started arguing loudly, both from the same mouth, and I woke up." She shudders, glancing down at the double-talking dog.

"What a dream!" Jerry stares thoughtfully. "Look at him now. Nothing but hound."

Lowey is sitting up perfectly. Jerry feeds him some sausage. "I think his, uh, doggieness is winning out, Mom."

"Maybe. But he played with the ball of yarn while I was making breakfast. I wonder what he'll do when we go to church?"

"Probably sleep," says Jerry. "He can do that no matter who's in charge."

The church is packed, and people are whispering anxiously.

Preacher Plutz gives a long sermon on Not Being Two-faced, and Jerry dozes. All of a sudden, he hears Eva Ning's name and the words "Our Lady of Mercy Hospital." He jerks himself awake.

"We are all God's children," the preacher is saying.

"And we must submit to His will." He pauses. "But let us humbly beseech the Lord's blessing. Let us all join together in silent prayer for Eva. May she recover quickly and be healthy again. Amen."

Suddenly, there's a rude eruption from one of the pews. It echoes loudly in the silent sanctuary.

Jerry turns his head. He sees Peter Wardly, with a red face, sitting beside his parents.

After the service, Jerry corners Peter.

"What happened, man? Was that you?"

Peter squirms. "Yeah. I had to yawn, and as soon as my mouth was open, a big burp came blasting out. I couldn't stop it."

Jerry nods. "Bad timing. It seemed like a comment on Eva."

Peter looks ashamed. "I know. But I couldn't help it!"

"At least, she wasn't there," says Jerry. "And it wasn't a fart."

"Right." Peter smiles bitterly. "If I didn't know better, I'd think this happened because I'm thirteen. Ha ha."

When Jerry and his mother get home, Lowey greets them at the door. He barks happily.

At lunch, he sits up and begs. There's no sign of Jade.

"Maybe she's left," Jerry's mother says. "But I'm still going to talk with Sister Sorsy."

"Good luck." Jerry rolls his eyes. "I'll be down for supper. I've got a lot of homework."

When Jerry comes down for supper, Lowey greets him with a regular dog bark. His mother is sitting at the kitchen table, holding her head.

"Mom, are you all right?"

"Just another little spell. I took two pills this time." She smiles. "Sister Sorsy says Jade is still here, maybe lying low. She's still using Lowey as an agent." Her eyes grow wide. "But listen to this. Your father's spirit *knows* that Jade has been using Lowey, and he liked the idea of using an agent. So he entered . . . a mouse!

Jerry gapes in disbelief. "That's really too much, Mom."

"Well, Sister Sorsy was absolutely certain. "Just think about it. Lowey was already *taken,* so to speak, and there were no other suitable beings around. Beings with eyes, I mean. So it's all very logical. Remember: Sister Sorsy was right about Jade. So now—" she slams her forehead. "Oh, no! Lowey caught a mouse this afternoon!"

Jerry stares. Horrified, they gape into each other's eyes.

"What happened, Mom? Lowey didn't kill the mouse, did he?"

"No, I don't think so." She thinks back, wildly. "He

pinned the mouse's tail against the floor with his paw." She gasps. "I said *Good boy, Lowey*. Oh, how could I have said that?" She wildly gnashes her teeth. "I was praising him for catching your father!"

Jerry gulps. "What happened then, Mom?"

"I'm trying to think. Oh, I remember. My praise distracted Lowey. The mouse wiggled free and scampered down the cellar stairs." She sighs with relief.

Jerry closes the cellar door to keep Lowey out. "I'll go to see Wilcox tomorrow. Right after school."

His mother nods. "Good idea. The mouse may have another way of entering the kitchen. Mice don't need a big crack, you know. Mercy me! If Lowey catches that mouse again, I hope your father gets out in time."

Up in his room, Jerry reviews the situation. Peter is cured, but now his dad is using a mouse as an agent! How long will this last? According to Sister Sorsy, Jade is still haunting Lowey. And his mother's dizziness seems to be getting worse.

Jerry sits in meditation. He makes his mind a blank. He goes deeply into the Stillness. He tries to connect with his Higher Self. He really needs some guidance now!

Jerry sits for a long time. He prays for his mother.

All of a sudden, he remembers what Wilcox said about cheating karma. Even if you manage to help somebody avoid bad karma, it will strike anyway, in some other form.

With a jolt, Jerry realizes that maybe he's praying for his mother to cheat her karma! He resolves to ask Wilcox about it.

EIGHT

MONDAY morning, Willie tells a new joke: "How does Doofus lock his front door at night? He double locks it for safety by turning the key first one way and then the other. Goofus is smarter. He locks his door from the outside to make sure nobody can get in."

Hardly anyone laughs. The kids are all whispering about Eva. She has a terrible disease, and it could be fatal. No one mentions Peter's ill-timed burp.

But Peter isn't gloomy any more. It's a miracle! He didn't even bring his little blue bag of good-luck charms to school. As Willie says, he's finally stopped being "snooperstitious."

When they flock into English class, there's a grinning cat on the blackboard. Jerry recognizes it from *Alice in Wonderland,* but it makes him think of Jade.

Mr. Stim, the eighth-grade English teacher, is a handsome man with sly, half-open eyes. The girls call them "bedroom eyes," and some of them have a crush on him.

Mr. Stim prides himself on "stretching young minds." He's a pretty good artist, and he likes to challenge his students with difficult concepts and ideas.

Every Monday, Mr. Stim draws something on the blackboard. Then he asks probing questions until the kids can't stand it any longer. At that point, they start talking and have what he calls "a tantalizing discussion."

Last week, he drew a stack of dollar bills. Then he talked about "philanthropy" (What is the *best* way to help the poor?). The week before, he sketched a bottle with a skull and crossbones on it. Then he talked about "euthanasia" (Is it *ever* justifiable to put a dying person out of his/her misery?).

Strangely enough, the best "tantalizing discussions" have been about Happiness and Revenge. ("What is true happiness?" and "Is there really such a thing as revenge?")

Now, Mr. Stim grins like the cat on the blackboard. It's a sly, smirky grin. He writes "SCHRÖDINGER'S CAT" on the board in capital letters. Below that, he draws a box and writes: "The Uncertainty Principle."

"Good morning, my friends," he says. "Suppose there's a cat in this box, together with a device that may or may not poison it. Is the cat dead or alive?"

He narrows his sleepy eyes. "That is uncertain. The only way to be sure is to open the box and look. Does anyone wish to comment?"

Jerry's been thinking about Jade. Then he remembers what Wilcox said, years ago, about a tree in the forest. He waves his hand.

"Yes, Jerry?"

"Nothing is real unless we perceive it."

Mr. Stim's eyes grow wide. "Interesting! Nothing is real . . . unless we perceive it. Where did you get that idea?"

"Uh, from a friend."

"Well, what would *you yourself* say? Think carefully, Mr. Shore, because I'm going to give you a very real grade for your answer."

Laughter ripples across the room.

Uh-oh. Jerry squirms. Why did he raise his hand? Wait! What did Wilcox say?

"Well, Jerry? Our waiting for you to speak is also very real."

Jerry silently chokes. He can't recall exactly what Wilcox said. "Uh, if a tree falls in the forest, and there's nobody there to hear it, there's, uh, nothing to hear. I mean, nothing heard. I mean . . ."

Muffled giggles. Jerry turns red. Suzie is there too!

Mr. Stim fingers his chin. He seems to take pity on Jerry. "This isn't as easy as it might seem. Let's get someone else involved. Yes. Willie Fielder."

Willie lowers the arm he's been waving. "Even if you're not there, you could set up a recording machine, to record the sound."

"Right!" Mr. Stim exclaims. "But would the recording be real, if no one listened to it?" He gives Willie a penetrating look.

Jerry almost raises his hand. He just remembered what Wilcox said. *Someone has to create the sound by hearing it. Your thoughts and senses are like a pair of spectacles. Take them off, and no one knows what's what.*

Willie is stammering now. "I, uh, I guess the recording would be real, if the recording machine is."

"Aha!" Mr. Stim holds up a long finger. "But is the machine real, if no one is there to perceive it?"

"I, uh . . ." Willie makes a small choking sound. "I don't think . . ."

"Maybe you *should* think." Mr. Stim chuckles. "In fact, thinking might be helpful for all of us. We shall revisit the uncertain cat later. Now please open your books to the poem you studied for today." He clears his throat. "Your assignment, by the way, is to read Chapter Eleven. "I mention this now because when the bell rings, some of you blast away like rockets."

After school, Jerry goes straight to see Wilcox. The old man is sitting quietly before his cardboard house. He greets Jerry with his eyes still closed.

"Wilcox! I need your help." Jerry sits down beside him.

"I'll do my best." The old man opens his eyes. "What's happening?"

"Lowey is haunted."

Wilcox looks puzzled. "Who's Lowey? I'm seeing a dog."

"Yes, our new basset hound. Mom says that Sister Sorsy said that after Jade died, her spirit entered the puppy. Is that possible?"

"The cat's spirit, or Sister Sorsy's?"

Jerry laughs. Wilcox can make anything fun. "Jade's. Lowey sometimes acts like a cat."

Wilcox thinks for a minute. "Well, I've never heard of that happening. I think it's more likely that Jade's spirit hovered around you and your mother. After that, she may have been *reborn* as a puppy . . . but if that's the case, her memories are astonishingly strong. She should get used to being a dog soon."

Jerry twitches excitedly. "Sister Sorsy says my dad's spirit entered a mouse. Could that be true?" He suddenly shudders and gulps. "Or could my dad have been reborn . . . that way?"

Wilcox says nothing. His eyes glaze over with a distant look. He sits quietly for several minutes. Then he snaps his head and blinks. "I don't think any of that has happened with your father, Jerry."

Jerry sighs with relief. "I didn't really believe it." He frowns. "But I'm worried about my mom. Her dizzy spells are getting worse. And Eva Ning is really sick. Preacher Plutz asked everyone to pray for her. I've been praying hard for Mom and Eva both."

Wilcox gives him a compassionate look. "That's a lot of worry, a lot of stress. "I think it's time you learned The Smile."

"The Smile?"

"Yes. If the eyes, as they say, are a window onto the soul, The Smile can be a door into serenity."

Jerry likes the sound of that. "How does it work?"

As if in illustration, Wilcox himself smiles. "The Smile is peace-bringing. When you do it correctly, your worries and tensions fade away."

"I'd like that," says Jerry.

"All right. Let's give it a try. Keep sitting just like that. Let yourself totally relax. Try to get in tune, in touch with your Higher Self. Picture yourself in total mastery of your life."

Jerry does his best.

"Good. Now picture a smooth, quiet lake on a warm summer day. Breathe deeply and slowly, smiling gently. If you do that successfully, your smile will be calm and peaceful, even triumphant."

Jerry breathes and smiles.

"Very good. Your only focus is on your relaxed body, your serene smile. Keep out any invading thoughts.

Everything feels light and effortless. Your smile will now become radiant. Excellent!"

Jerry feels at peace. "I'm doing it right," he says proudly.

"Careful. Down, Ego, down!" Wilcox grins. "But you've got it. All you need to do is practice."

"Thanks, Wilcox. I feel a lot better."

"Of course you do. Smiling is healthy."

"Why?"

"Exercising the smile muscles is very beneficial."

That night, Jerry practices The Smile for a long time. As he falls asleep, he seems to be floating on a calm, quiet lake.

NINE

THE NEXT morning, Jerry's mother makes poached eggs on toast with marmalade. She opens a can of tuna for Lowey.

The puppy sits up to beg perfectly now, his eyes sparkling. But when he whines, it still sounds more like a meow.

Jerry listens carefully. "Wilcox thinks Jade may have been *reborn* as Lowey, Mom."

His mother smiles sweetly. "He's a nice man, dear. But he doesn't even have a crystal ball, does he?"

Lowey starts hissing and dancing. He looks confused, squirming like he wants to jump out of his skin. He runs in clumsy circles, growling and chasing himself.

"That does it." Jerry's mother clanks down the tuna can. "We're taking that dog to the vet for a check-up."

Jerry gulps. "Is that smart, Mom?"

"Well, this can't go on forever. The inner struggle will kill him!" She paradoxically feeds the dog an extra bite of tuna. "I'll call and make an appointment. You come straight home after school."

In English class, Mr. Stim makes a joke about "the cat's pajamas" that no one understands. Then he wonders if anyone has solved the problem. He talks about "The Uncertainty Principle." Jerry keeps his mouth shut this time, and no one else volunteers.

At recess, Willie tells another "D and G joke" (as they are now called): "When Doofus finds a good fishing spot in the lake, he carefully makes an X on the side of the boat so he can locate it later. Goofus is smarter. He leaves his tackle box floating there."

This one gets a few weak laughs, even a giggle from Suzie.

After school, Jerry goes directly home, as instructed. Suzie comes with him to see the new puppy.

When they enter the kitchen, Lowey is crouching beside the stove. He looks anxious and afraid, like a fox cornered by hounds.

"Aw," says Suzie. "He's so cute!"

"Hello, Suzie," says Jerry's mom.

"Hi, Mrs. Shore!" Suzie runs over and hugs the cowering dog.

"We're taking him to the vet for a check-up," Jerry tells her. "He seems to sense that something is up, Mom."

"I couldn't keep it from him." His mother sighs. "He's smart as a whip! Could you and Suzie please walk him, Jerry? Our appointment with Dr. Kurr is in forty minutes. We don't want any accidents when he's on the table."

"Sure, Mom. C'mon, boy."

They circle the big pine several times, but the walk is not successful. Suzie inveigles the puppy into fetching a few pinecones.

When they return, it's time to leave.

Jerry's mother drives. Sitting beside her, Jerry holds Lowey in his lap. The puppy looks anxiously out the window, slobbering on the glass.

"Remember now. Not a word about the haunting!"

"Okay, Mom."

When they arrive, the tall, dark-haired vet is bending over a plump lady behind the front desk. He wears a crisp, white coat. His thin, black mustache curls across his cheeks like tiny twin snakes.

Dr. Kurr whispers something to the plump lady. They both snicker.

Jerry approaches, holding Lowey in his arms, his mother just behind.

"Oh, I didn't see you there, sonny." The doctor's face turns red.

"We have an appointment," Jerry's mother declares. "This is Lohengrin. We call him Lowey."

"Of course, Mrs. Shore." Dr. Kurr smiles. "I'm so sorry about Jade, but there was nothing we could do. Come right this way, please."

He leads them to a small, cream-colored room. The walls are covered with cutesy photos of cats and dogs.

Jerry hikes Lowey up onto the examination table. The puppy makes a soft, catlike sound. Jerry tenses. Did the doctor notice?

Dr. Kurr pats Lowey on the head. "Good boy. That's quite a replacement, Mrs. Shore! What seems to be the trouble?"

Jerry holds his breath.

"Nothing, really," says Jerry's mom, yawning a bit too casually. "I bought him recently, and I was hoping you'll check him out. He does seem a little . . . high-strung." Grabbing her head, she slumps down onto a chair.

Dr. Kurr rushes over. "Are you all right, Mrs. Shore?"

"Oh, yes. Just a little tired."

"A glass of water, perhaps?"

"No, thank you. I sometimes get these little dizzy spells. Please go right ahead."

"As you wish." Dr. Kurr pokes and pries the puppy,

listens to his heart. He even shoves a thermometer in his butt. Lowey takes it all pretty well. He crouches, and the doctor deftly holds a paper towel beneath his rear end.

Depositing the bulging towel in a trash receptacle, he turns to Jerry's mom. "A perfectly healthy dog, Mrs. Shore. In fact, he . . ."

Arching his back, Lowey gives a spectacular imitation of a hissing teakettle.

Dr. Kurr gapes. "My word! That *is* rather unusual behavior." He bends down, cautiously looking into the puppy's eyes. "Ssss? Ssss?"

They awkwardly bump noses. Lowey suspiciously sniffs. He seems completely normal again.

The doctor shines his light into Lowey's nose and throat. He shrugs. "I see no obstruction. Sometimes a new pet acts a little strangely. Nothing to worry about. Let's let sleeping dogs lie, heh heh."

Jerry is really stressed out! He's worried about his mom and nervous about Jade. He decides to use The Smile. He thinks of his Higher Self. He pictures a calm, peaceful lake. He breathes slowly and deeply, smiling faintly. He envisions himself in total mastery of his life.

The Smile is peaceful, with a touch of triumph. It is also subtly suggestive, as if Jerry knows a well-kept secret.

Dr. Kurr shudders, turning pale. *Curses! That boy*

must have heard me charging Mrs. Flathers double! He's thinking of blabbing. A bright-red coloration spreads across his face.

"Well, thank you for coming, Mrs. Shore. I know you're still grieving about Jade, so this first visit with, um, Lowey is absolutely free." He gives Jerry an earnest, meaningful stare. "Absolutely *free.* It was a great pleasure to examine such a healthy animal."

He pats the puppy, who hisses softly.

Jerry keeps smiling. He feels so much better now!

TEN

THE NEXT morning, in school, Willie proudly announces that he has a new D and G joke. "How does Doofus tie his shoes?" he asks loudly. Some kids groan, but nobody knows.

Grinning smugly, Willie puts one foot on the seat of his desk and reaches down to tie the other shoe on the floor. Monty smiles, but nobody laughs.

"Goofus is smarter," Willie declares. "He ties both his shoes before he puts them on."

Nobody laughs at all.

"I think your uncle Mort has run out of good ones," Cromer Borkin remarks. "They never were that good, anyway."

Willie shrugs. "Not everyone has the brains to appreciate true wit."

"Oh, yeah?" Cromer makes a fist, but Mr. Stim opens the door. "Well, I see we're all cramming for the pop quiz," he says cheerfully.

Books fly open all around the room.

After school, Jerry goes straight to see Wilcox. The old man sits calmly before his simple cardboard dwelling.

"Hi Jerry." He opens his eyes. "I hope things are going better."

"Yes, thank you." Jerry sits down. "And thank you for The Smile. I used it when we took Lowey to the vet."

Wilcox nods. "Is the dog still acting like a cat?"

"Yes, but Dr. Kurr didn't seem worried, even when Lowey hissed." Jerry laughs. "But The Smile really helped me!"

"I'm glad. Do it any time you feel stressed. Or any time at all. Surrender your fears and anxieties. Let them be replaced by a strong faith that all will be well if you let go of your little ego."

"Thanks. I was, uh, just wondering . . . If I pray for my mom to get well, am I helping her to cheat her karma, like you said about Peter?"

"Good thinking. But don't forget about the X-factor, Divine Grace. If you manage to reach your Higher Self, your prayer might be granted. It takes time and work, of course, for that to happen. Still, you've been treading the path for a good three years now. Bad karma is a complex, powerful force, but it can be changed."

"My Higher Self . . . can do that?"

"Oh, yes. Easy as pie! So it's all right to pray for someone. But you should pray for what is *best* for that person, even though you have no idea what the best really is. Then you're not praying for them to cheat their karma."

"Thanks. I'll pray for my mom that way. Eva Ning too."

"Have you heard what's wrong with her?"

"Not yet. But she's in the hospital. On Sunday, Preacher Plutz asked everyone to pray for her."

Wilcox flinches slightly. "It would be good to pray for *the best* for her too. But don't take it too hard if she leaves us."

Jerry feels horror prickles. "You mean she might die?"

Wilcox thinks for a few moments. Then he gives Jerry a compassionate look. "I don't know, of course, but I sense that she might." He sighs. "But in some ways, death is a blessing. It is good that we are released from the "physical tomb," as Plato put it, and then reborn. Without death, think what the world would become. Too crowded to turn around!"

Jerry ponders this. "I see what you mean."

Wilcox looks very serious. "If you devote this life to trying to merge with your Higher Self, it will greatly benefit you at death. My teacher used to quote the Russian writer Tolstoy, who said that dying without regret or fear is the greatest possible deed in this life."

Jerry whistles. "Greater than any other deed?"

Wilcox smiles. "Well, perhaps such a death is only possible after a series of other great deeds, such as helping others and trying to find your Higher Self." He thinks for a moment. "Tibetans believe that it's very important how a person dies. At the time of death, you are already heading towards your next rebirth. Life is a preparation for death, just as death is a preparation for coming back.

"So it never ends?"

Wilcox smiles. "*Never* is longer than that. But Nature is very patient."

Jerry contemplates this. "I wonder why Eva has to die so young. Hey! Could you see . . . any of *her* past lives?"

Wilcox hesitates. "I might be able to, through her connection with you. Perhaps that will help you to help her in some way."

Closing his eyes, Wilcox sits in silence for several minutes. His upper body sways slightly. Finally, jerking his head, he opens his eyes. "In a past life, Eva was a concubine for the king of a country like ancient Persia."

Jerry looks puzzled. "Concubine?"

"Like a wife. But in a harem."

Jerry smiles. "I know what *that* is."

"Well, she was in the king's harem. But she also had a lover on the side."

Jerry is still marveling. "The King of Persia!"

"I said a country *like* Persia. Actually, I think this happened on another planet."

"Another planet!" Jerry's eyes bug out.

"Yes, in a distant solar system. One of the other concubines told the king about Eva and her lover. The king had both the offenders . . . tortured and put to death. Her lover had a drug to numb the pain, but he took it all himself."

Jerry grimaces. "Hey! If she was betrayed, maybe that's why it was easy for Mr. Flog to make her one of his spies. She wanted to betray someone else. Suzie said that Eva told Mr. Flog about the poem I wrote . . . making fun of him. I almost got paddled or whipped!"

Wilcox nods. "There may well be that connection. But karma is very complex. Many things acting together."

He looks into Jerry's eyes. "Can you forgive Eva? *Completely* forgive her? I think it would help you both. I sense a strong connection between you."

"I . . . I guess so."

"Good. First, you must ask forgiveness for your own past errors. You must surrender your ego. Then your anger will be erased."

Jerry whistles. "I'll try my best."

"Excellent. As Alexander Pope put it, messing up is human, but to forgive is divine."

"But how should I forgive Eva? Write to her? Tell her?"

Wilcox doesn't answer. Instead, he enters another trance. Soon, in a slightly different voice, he says: "If you are helpless what to do, your Higher Self will see you through." Snapping his head, he opens his eyes.

"Uh, what does that mean, exactly?"

"I think you know, Jerry. Open your heart. Turn to your Higher Self for Inspiration and Guidance. But remember to be sure your intentions are pure. And don't forget The Smile."

Jerry grins. "I won't. Thanks, Wilcox!"

ELEVEN

"GRUFF! WOOF!" When Jerry gets home, Lowey greets him with purely canine salutations.

"Hi Jerry!" His mother emerges from the kitchen. "Lowey is nothing but basset hound now. Sister Sorsy saw Jade's spirit slipping away. She called it *vacating the premises*. And you won't believe this!"

"What, Mom?"

"Jade has *already* been reborn . . . as a fisherman in China. You know how she loved fish."

"What!"

"You heard me. A fisherman in China. Sister Sorsy saw it in her crystal ball."

"She has China in her crystal ball?"

"Very funny. Sister Sorsy says your father has also moved on. But he just turned down a chance for rebirth as a fierce warrior in a remote section of Africa, so he still might come back to watch over us. Eva Ning, by the way, will make a complete and full recovery."

"That's good, Mom. Could we have supper a little late? I want to visit Eva at the hospital."

"That's nice, dear. I'll keep a plate warm for you. But isn't it past visiting hours?"

"I'll, uh, try to talk my way in. I really want to see her." Jerry is thinking hard. *I can use The Look if I have to.*

"Want me to drive you?"

"No thanks. I'll jog. I need the exercise."

It's already dark twilight when Jerry hits the front walk, breathing heavily. He can barely read the sign: OUR LADY OF MERCY HOSPITAL. The building looms gray and forbidding, reminding him of a gloomy prison. He pushes open the heavy front door, marches straight to the reception desk.

A thin lady with bright-red hair is transferring little packages from her desk drawer to her purse. Startled, she looks up at Jerry. "Sorry. Visiting hours are over. I was just leaving."

"Please. I need to see Eva Ning. It's urgent."

The lady hastily zips up her purse. "Are you related to the patient?"

Jerry hesitates. "Uh, no, but—"

"Only immediate family after visiting hours."

Jerry grimaces. This is so frustrating! Should he use The Look?

A wave of stress hits him hard. He thinks of his Higher Self. He pictures a peaceful lake, imagines himself in total mastery of his life. He breathes deeply, smiling faintly.

The Smile is peaceful, mysteriously knowing, and triumphant.

The red-haired lady twitches. *Uh-oh. He saw me slipping those drugs into my purse.*

She gives Jerry a crafty look, like they're conspirators in a sinister crime. "Well, I'm authorized to make exceptions . . . in special cases. You seem like the sort of young man who can keep a secret. You *are*, aren't you?"

"Oh, yes," says Jerry. He feels much better now.

"But Eva is a very sick girl. Any excitement could be harmful."

Jerry nods gratefully. "I understand. Thank you!"

"Just go right up. She's in room 403. I know she'll be happy to see you. And remember our little secret."

"Yes, ma'am!"

When Jerry steps off the elevator, a sharp, antiseptic smell assaults his nostrils. He checks the numbers on the doors, goes the wrong way, and wheels around, arriving at 403.

He swings the door quietly open. The room is a ghastly white, lit by a soft light beside the bed. Large, standing machines blink and whir, but Jerry's eyes go right to Eva.

She's lying in a white bed, propped up on two pillows, pale covers drawn up to her chin. She's wired to some of the machines. Her face is thin, haggard, drawn. Her eyes stare sadly out of deep, shadowy holes.

A supper tray, untouched, sits on a swinging ledge beside the bed.

"Eva!"

"Hi, Jerry. How did you get here?" She groans in pain.

"The elevator. How do you feel, Eva? You, uh, look pretty good."

"Liar." She has a brief coughing fit. It's a hacking, croaky cough. Reaching out with a bony hand, she coughs into an open tissue.

Jerry glimpses a bright red splotch before she folds it up.

Eva grimaces, clutching her chest. "I'm really glad you came, Jerry. My parents left for dinner . . . but they'll be back soon." Her voice is weak, hollow, shaky.

Jerry tries not to gape. Eva looks like a living skeleton. He prays for the best for her. His eyes grow misty. "I, uh, just wanted to say . . ."

"Yes?"

Jerry hesitates. He hasn't *completely* forgiven Eva yet. Maybe it's too soon to say so. His intentions wouldn't be totally pure. *If you are helpless what to do, your Higher Self will see you through.*

There's a soft knock on the door, and it swings open.

Eva's parents come in. "Oh, hello, Jerry," her mother says. "Doesn't she look well?"

"Uh, yeah, sure, Mrs. Ning."

Mr. Ning shakes Jerry's hand. "Thanks for coming, son. How did you get in here?"

"I, uh, did some fast talking." Jerry smiles.

"Well, we're so glad you came," says Mrs. Ning. "Eva was very energetic this morning." She frowns at the untouched tray. "Ate a good breakfast too, didn't you, dear?" She pushes Jerry gently towards the door. "She's much better now. Thank you so much for coming. I'll bet you haven't even had your own supper yet."

Jerry feels himself pushed firmly towards the door.

"'Bye, Eva," he says. "I'll come to see you on Saturday."

TWELVE

JERRY jogs all the way home. When he walks in the door, Lowey barks happily. It's totally doglike. Not a trace of Jade.

"Your plate is in the oven," his mother says. "I'll get it."

Jerry sits at the table, attacking hunks of fried chicken, mashed potatoes, and string beans. All that jogging made him ravenous. He slips Lowey a juicy piece of dark meat.

"Make sure there aren't any bones, dear. How was Eva?"

Jerry empties a glass of cold milk. "Not good, Mom." He sighs. "I'm afraid she doesn't have much . . ."

"That's what I've heard, honey. But it's only a rumor. Sister Sorsy said she'll be fine. But it was sweet of you to visit her."

"Mrs. Ning kept insisting she was better, but she looked awful. I'm going back on Saturday. If she still . . ." All of a sudden, tears start streaming down his cheeks.

Jerry's mother stares, wide-eyed. "It's all right to be sensitive, dear. But remember, everyone has to go sometime. At least, *Suzie* is still in good health."

Sitting at his desk, Jerry pushes his homework away. He thinks about Eva and her grandfather, the lion tamer, whose head got crushed in a lion's mouth. That was a gruesome death, but probably quick. He remembers how, *after Eva told on him,* he sat on a hard wooden chair in Mr. Flog's office, sweating like a pig, terrified of getting paddled or whipped.

Then he thinks of Eva in her hospital bed, coughing up blood, looking like death itself. Her shadowy, staring eyes, sunk so deep in her face. The terrible fear and pain she must be feeling . . .

Like Wilcox said, Jerry asks for forgiveness of his own past errors. He tries to surrender his ego. He works hard to erase *all* his anger. To forgive Eva completely. He prays to his Higher Self. For a long time, he prays for what is best for Eva. *I think it would help you both.*

After a while, a murky picture of a man begins to form in Jerry's mind.

Suddenly there's a big thud, like something heavy

hitting the floor. Lowey's frantic barking echoes from below.

"Mom! Are you okay?"

No answer.

He gallops down the stairs, two at a time.

His mother is sprawled in the dark hallway, holding her head. "I'm so dizzy, Jerry. I just couldn't stand up."

Jerry shudders. "What can I do, Mom? Can you sit up? Wait, I'll bring you a pillow."

She laughs bravely. "Oh, I'll be all right." She forces herself to her feet, holding onto the wall. "See? Nothing's broken. I'll just need to be a little more careful. You go back and finish your homework."

The next day is a non-stop nightmare. Jerry's mother is too dizzy to walk. Dr. Trainer gives her some stronger pills, but they hardly help at all. She crawls on her hands and knees to use the bathroom.

Jerry stays home from school. He sits with his mother, praying for what is best. He brings her hot soup, but she waves it away. He feeds puppy biscuits to Lowey, munches dry Wheaties himself.

Jerry's mother calls up Sister Sorsy, asking for advice. A few minutes later, Sister Sorsy calls back. Her crystal ball has revealed three evil spirits, drinking up Jerry's mother's life force, "like blood in three goblets." She advises chanting a mantra: "Evil spirits, where thou art, hear me please and then depart."

The mantra doesn't seem to help, even though Jerry's mother makes him chant it too.

Early Friday morning, a heavy nurse in a white uniform, Mrs. Broonlik, comes early so that Jerry can go to school. She looks like a grinning witch.

Jerry sat up almost all night with his mother, so he sleepwalks through his classes, bleary-eyed.

In the hallway just before English class, Jerry sees Mr. Stim coming out of the faculty supply closet. Smiling slyly, he firmly shuts the door.

"Mr. Stim, I'm afraid I wasn't able to finish my composition last night. You see—"

"I'm sorry, Jerry." The teacher shakes his head. "I assigned that a long time ago."

"But my mom is sick, and I've been . . ."

"That's an old excuse!" Mr. Stim snaps.

Jerry feels extremely stressed. He thinks of his Higher Self. He pictures a calm, quiet lake. He imagines himself in total mastery of his life. He breathes slowly, smiling faintly.

The Smile is peaceful, yet uncannily knowing and triumphant.

Mr. Stim sways unsteadily. He tries to tell himself that Jerry can't possibly *know*, but the boy's smile proves otherwise. *How in blazes? He must have seen us together and figured it out.* Mr. Stim pretends to sneeze into his handkerchief, but actually wipes his lips and examines the square of white linen. There is no sign of lipstick.

"Wait, Jerry. Perhaps I was a bit hasty."

"Hasty?"

"Yes, my lad. As a matter of fact, you've been doing excellent work." Mr. Stim gives Jerry a significant wink. "You may forget about that composition. I'll just jot down the A-plus you would no doubt have received." He winks again. "But this will be our little *secret*. A secret between good friends. All right?"

"Yes, sir. Good friends. Absolutely."

"Excellent."

Together, the good friends amble toward Mr. Stim's classroom. Jerry fails to see the supply-closet door, behind them, slowly open. Miss Joy Pertlet, the shapely young school secretary, emerges. She locks the door with her key and walks away.

When Jerry gets home, he learns that his mother has arranged for another nurse, Mrs. March, to come at night. She looks like a meek, white-haired lamb.

Mrs. March is gentle and helpful, but Jerry is too wound-up to sleep. He does The Smile to relieve his stress. He prays to his Higher Self for guidance. He prays for what is "best" for his mom, desperately hoping there's a little "wiggle room" between what is best and cheating her karma.

THIRTEEN

EARLY Saturday morning, Jerry looks out the window. Masses of dark-gray clouds roll ominously across the sky. It begins to rain. *Great! I'll get drenched when I go to see Eva.*

To make matters worse, his mother is feeling terrible. She says she's all right, but Jerry notices that her dizziness is worse. She can't even turn her head on the pillow without groaning and clenching her eyes.

She probably needs to see a specialist, but he remembers what she said about *them*. Still, Dr. Trainer seems to be no help at all. Between bites of softly popping Rice Krispies, Jerry does The Smile. Thank heavens for that!

Witch-like Mrs. Broonlik replaces meek Mrs. March.

Jerry puts on his slick yellow rain gear. Walking to the hospital, he's lashed by slanting, fitful squalls. For just a moment, the glowing sun shines through, only to drown like a red-capped swimmer in a stormy sea.

The hospital stands like a gloomy gray fortress. There's nobody at the reception desk. Jerry piles his dripping rain gear on a chair and takes the elevator to the fourth floor.

Eva's mother springs up when Jerry enters. "Shush! She's sleeping now, and needs her rest. But she's much better, she is."

Jerry nods. He can see Eva lying in bed behind her mother. Her eyes are closed, and her mouth is open. She looks very frail and weak. Beside the bed is an untouched breakfast tray.

Eva's father stands at the window, his arms folded across his chest. "Hello, Jerry." He mouths the words.

"Hi, Mr. Ning," Jerry whispers.

Eva's mother seizes his arm. "She was very energetic this morning," she whispers. A tear rolls down her face. "Ate a little breakfast too. She's much better now. But sometimes the pain is bad. They've given her morphine. Can you please watch over her while we get a bite to eat at the cafeteria? There's supposed to be a nurse, but they're short-handed today."

"Sure thing, Mrs. Ning." *Why did I make that stupid rhyme?*

"If there's any trouble, just push the button on the

end of this cord by the bed. But I'm sure there won't be. She's better today."

As soon as they leave, Eva opens her eyes.

"Hi, Jerry." She scrunches up her face in pain.

"Eva! You're awake."

"Yeah." She groans. "I just couldn't stand their cheerful pep-talks any longer."

Jerry edges closer. "I hope it's not too bad."

She makes a bitter laugh. "Only like jagged knives, sawing me apart." Her breath has a sour, metallic smell.

Jerry remembers what Wilcox said: *There may well be that connection.* He takes a deep breath. "Eva, I wanted to tell you . . . I forgive you for telling Mr. Flog about the poem I wrote last year."

Eva's eyes grow wide. "No! I never— Wait, who told you?" Her lips are trembling. "Who?" She coughs sharply, painfully, snatches up a tissue, thinks for a second. "It was Suzie, wasn't it?"

Jerry smiles sadly. "It doesn't matter, Eva. What matters is that I forgive you. I truly, honestly forgive you with all my heart."

Eva shudders. A tear rolls down her cheek. "Thank you," she breathes. "I'm sorry, Jerry."

He's about to say something, when her troubled face goes peaceful and serene. "I'm sorry to you," she whispers. "And I'm sorry to my mama and papa. Please tell them if . . . Ooh! It's getting worse. I need more morphine, Jerry." She gropes for the bell-cord, presses the button.

Jerry prays to his Higher Self for guidance. He prays for the best for Eva.

She cries and moans. She tears at her hair, screams with pain.

A nurse appears at the door.

"Eva needs more morphine," says Jerry.

The nurse bites her lip. "The doctor said that any more . . . would be dangerous," she whispers to Jerry. "I'm so sorry. There's nothing I can do. But there are two other patients I *can* help, who need me." She slips out the door.

Eva writhes in pain. "I heard. That traitor!"

Jerry stands beside the bed. He's in agony, watching Eva suffer.

She quiets down again. Her face looks tense, like she's fighting terrible pain.

"I need to sleep now," she says through gritted teeth. "Please leave me, Jerry." She manages a weak smile.

What should he do? She's obviously trying not to scream again. What would Wilcox say? *Your Higher Self will see you through.*

"All right," Jerry says. "I hope you feel better soon."

Saying a quick prayer, he quietly leaves. But for some reason, he lingers in the hall just outside her door. Something isn't right. He tries not to cry. His throat is all choked up.

Total silence. He concentrates. His lips move slowly. His heart is wide open. He asks his Higher Self for guidance.

The crash is muffled, but he hears it clearly. Jerry's eyes widen. The skin on his arms prickles. Somehow, he *knows*.

Swinging open the door, he sees Eva holding a long shard of glass, moving it purposely toward her throat.

Jerry rushes to the bed. "Eva! No! Look at me."

She pauses, startled for a brief moment. But it's enough. Jerry looks deeply into her wild, sunken eyes.

Tension drains from her face. She slumps back against the pillows. The hand with the shard falls down beside her.

"You will lie peacefully."

"Lie peacefully."

Jerry holds her eyes with The Look. Inside him, a wave of painful compassion arises. He remembers what Wilcox said about not cheating karma. And about Eva's past life: *Her lover had a drug to numb the pain, but took it all himself.*

Jerry grimaces. *Eva has suffered enough, hasn't she?* He shouts the words inside his head. *HASN'T SHE?*

"Listen, Eva. The pain is gone."

"Gone." She smiles faintly. "Gone."

"Yes. And you'll never feel it again."

"Never . . . feel it again." Her expression is beautiful now.

We need to put the pieces of glass on your tray."

Some of the jagged shards are stuck in her napkin, which she'd wrapped around the glass when she smashed it.

"On my tray."

"Yes." Standing beside the bed, Jerry helps her do it. Tears of relief stream down his face.

Eva breathes evenly, deeply. Several seconds pass.

Jerry wipes his cheek. Has he done the right thing? He hopes so. He thinks so. He's grateful to his Higher Self.

The nurse steps in. "I thought I heard . . . But she's resting peacefully. Yes, I can see that. She seems better."

Jerry nods. "The pain was terrible." He can barely talk.

"Yes, but now . . ." She stares. "This drinking glass is broken!"

"Good morning, Nurse Bidgin. How is Eva doing?" Doctor Freel stands in the open door.

"She's better," Jerry blurts. "Eva is feeling fine now."

"Fine now." Eva smiles happily.

The doctor's eyes grow wide. "Why, that's wonderful! When did this happen, nurse?"

"I'm not sure. This boy was with her. I had to check on Mrs. Flint, and when I came back . . ."

"Well, this is amazing. Let me examine you, dear."

Eva stares straight ahead, still smiling.

Jerry leans closer. "The doctor wants to have a look."

"Have a look."

Doctor Freel looks suspicious. "How strange! This girl is acting like she's under hypnosis." He reaches out to take her hand.

As he touches Eva, she makes a long sigh. Her head flops sideways on the pillow. Her eyes lock vaguely onto the ceiling.

Nurse Bidgin crosses herself.

"Eva! Don't go. Please, don't." But Jerry knows she's already gone. He can feel it. He can see it. He stands helplessly beside the bed, praying for the best for her.

"We're back," says Eva's mother, opening the door. "How—"

Jerry silently shakes his head. He wipes the tears away.

"No!" Eva's mother rushes to the bed, frantically embracing the lifeless body. "No, no!"

Dr. Freel looks down at the floor.

Nurse Bidgin weeps.

Eva's father bows his head, his lips moving quickly. Then he turns to Jerry. "You must have been a very close friend. Closer than we knew."

Jerry nods. "She . . . asked me to tell you both . . . she was sorry."

"Good Lord! For what?"

"She didn't say."

FOURTEEN

SUNDAY dawns clear and warm. Jerry hardly slept at all, and the bright light cuts his eyes. It feels as if he has a sharp headache.

He brings his mother a cup of hot tea. Also a jumbled pile of overcooked poached eggs, but she waves the plate away. "You eat it, dear. You need to keep your strength up."

"What about *your* strength, Mom?"

"I don't need much strength to lie here. I can't eat anyway. The vertigo gives me those terrible dry heaves."

Jerry nods, fighting back tears. His mom is losing weight fast. Dr. Trainer can't help her, and she refuses to see a specialist.

In the kitchen, Jerry uses The Smile, but it only helps a little. He still feels terribly stressed and sad.

Idly munching the eggs, he prays for what is best for his mom.

Lowey sits up on his butt, whining softly. Jerry puts his nearly empty plate on the floor. The puppy eagerly sweeps his tongue all over it.

Jerry sighs. The universe has been slowly, relentlessly crumbling all around him. Long ago, his father. Then Jade. Then Eva. And now, his mom. He shudders.

Mrs. Broonlik arrives, grinning, to replace Mrs. March. She bustles about the bed, checking Jerry's mother's vital signs.

"Why don't you go to church, dear? You can pray for Eva's soul. I'll be fine here with Mrs. Broonlik."

"Ya, she vill." The witch's eyes gleam. Jerry secretly calls her Mrs. Broomstick.

"All right, Mom. I'll walk Lowey first."

The church is packed with sad-looking people. They talk in subdued whispers.

Preacher Plutz sighs. Scanning the congregation, he begins: "Eva Ning was a lovely, meek little lamb whose way was cut tragically short . . . for reasons we cannot know but must humbly respect. Eva passed away peacefully yesterday, and she will be sorely missed. The funeral service will be here on Wednesday at eleven o'clock. Mrs. Hodges will collect your generous donations for floral arrangements."

Meek little lamb? Jerry's eyes flash. Eva was one of Mr. Flog's spies! She snitched on him, but said she was sorry when he forgave her. *Passed away peacefully?* She suffered in horrible agony before he used The Look. The pain was so bad she tried to kill herself! Preacher Plutz doesn't know . . . what he doesn't know.

Jerry feels totally stressed out. He does The Smile. He prays for what is best for Eva, wherever she is. And for his mom too.

When the collection plate comes, he merely fluffs the dollar bills with his fingers. But then he changes his mind and puts in a dollar anyway.

Walking home, Jerry thinks about Death. He pictures it as a sinister creature in a black, hooded cape. It has a horrible, silent laugh. It doesn't carry a scythe, though. For some reason, this creature is even more terrible in bright daylight. And now, it's waiting for his mother.

He needs to see Wilcox!

Lowey happily greets him at the door. He seems to be hoping for more poached egg remains.

Mrs. Broonlik puts a finger to her lips. "Mrs. Shore, she is sleepink. Please be careful not to vake."

Jerry whispers back: "Thank you. I need to go out anyway, but I'll grab a bite first."

Trudging through the forest, Jerry does some telepathy.

Wilcox! Are you there?

Where else, Jerry? Are you all right?

I think so, but Eva died.

I'm sorry.

Thanks. But I forgave her.

Good.

Was I . . . the king or the lover?

The lover, I think.

I was afraid of that. I used The Look to stop her suffering.

That was kind.

I need your help now.

I'll do my best. Where are you?

I'll be there in ten minutes.

Sounds good.

FIFTEEN

WILCOX is sitting quietly as usual, but he jumps up when Jerry appears. He holds him by the shoulders. "You look a little haggard. Tell me what's been happening."

They sit face to face. Jerry wonders where to begin. "My mom is worse," he blurts. "She's wasting away. I can't bear . . . to lose her too."

"Whoa!" Wilcox put his arm around Jerry's shoulders. "Maybe it's not all that bad."

"She's so dizzy she has to crawl. She can't keep food down. She's getting so thin!" Jerry fights back tears. "Dr. Trainer's pills don't help anymore, and she won't see a specialist. There's a night nurse now, but I sit up with mom and pray. I don't know what else to do."

Wilcox nods sadly. "Take three deep breaths. That's right. Pull your shoulders up to your ears and let them drop. Good. Again. Now three more deep breaths."

Jerry feels better already. Wilcox is amazing!

"Listen, Jerry. There is only so much a person can do for someone else. Each of us walks our own path, and karma from the past can ripen at any time with lessons we've still to learn or apply. Our path leads to our Higher Self, but suffering teaches us along the way."

"But death is so unfair, so terrible!"

Wilcox nods. "Try to think of it this way. You had the good fortune to be born into a happy family. When your father died, the same wonderful karma that brought you together took him away. But only for the time being. He hasn't really been lost, and your Higher Self knows this. Your *minds* are still connected. Your strong love for him will act to bring you both together again somewhere, sometime." He smiles. "And if your mother goes—I'm not saying she will—the same thing will happen."

Jerry ponders this. Wilcox makes it sound so simple, so easy. But he hasn't seen how his mom is suffering!

Wilcox rubs Jerry's shoulders. "Don't quite believe me, do you?"

"No, I . . . guess I do. It's just that death is so sad."

"Remember what I said about living forever. The world would be a mess. Try to focus on being grateful for all the good times you've had." He rubs Jerry's shoulders again. "You're still a bit tense. Have you been using The Smile?"

"Oh, yes. And it helped a lot. It even seems to affect other people."

Wilcox smiles. "It does."

Jerry thinks back. "It worked with the lady at the hospital . . . and Mr. Stim, and Dr. Kurr. They *all* did something to help." His eyes grow wide. "Yes! It seemed to work like magic!"

"Hmm." Wilcox narrows his eyes. "Let me see you do The Smile again.

Jerry shows him.

Wilcox laughs and laughs. His whole body shakes. "No wonder! You're putting some of The Look into it. You're adding the part where you look as if you can see a person's innermost secrets! You aren't using the rest of The Look, so these people weren't hypnotized. But they must have felt guilty . . . about secrets you might have known."

Jerry thinks back. "Dr. Kurr was whispering something to the lady at the desk when I brought Lowey in. But I couldn't hear what he said." Jerry thinks some more. "The lady at the hospital was putting little boxes in her purse. I have no idea what Mr. Stim's secret was."

"Probably something devious." Wilcox laughs again. "When you first did The Smile with me, you didn't add any of The Look. It must have sneaked in later, when you practiced. And the results, evidently, were powerful."

Jerry nods. "I guess they were." He thinks for a

minute. "Hey! Could you see any of my mom's past lives, like you did with Peter and Eva?"

Wilcox hesitates. "All right. I'll try, through her connection with you." Closing his eyes, he goes into a deep trance. His upper body gently sways.

Jerry holds his breath. The only sound is an invisible bird, trilling in a distant tree.

Finally, Wilcox jerks his head, slowly opens his eyes. "I think I found what we need," he says. "Your mother was a rich landowner in ancient Russia. He used to drink vodka until he got dizzy. He allowed his peasants to starve while he himself guzzled vodka and ate huge dinners. It was a Let-them-eat-caviar sort of thing."

Jerry doesn't get the reference, but he clearly understands. "My mom would never have done that!"

Wilcox shrugs. "We have all done terrible things in past lives, as you now know."

Jerry shudders. "But she's always fed me so well!

Wilcox smiles. "Good. Think of that when you pray. Maybe that will help her to recover." He puts a hand on Jerry's shoulder. "Remember that karma is very complex. Our past lives influence us, yes, but there are many causes.

Jerry muses for a moment. "You said I was probably Eva's lover. But could you see into my other past lives?"

Wilcox nods. "I was wondering when you'd ask that. I've already tried to explore them." He pauses, gazing into the distance. "Here are some psychic impressions for what they're worth. Many lives ago, you were a monk who broke his vows and became a cardsharp. You were also a female acrobat, a successful male diplomat, and a shady lawyer. Then a great female healer, and a spiritual teacher."

Jerry's head is spinning. "I . . . I don't see how I can learn from all that."

Wilcox thinks for a moment. "Years ago, when you slid down that old drainpipe with The Doubler, you might have drawn upon your former agility as an acrobat. That was possible because you are *mind*. Mind, with its karma, continues in a rebirth."

Jerry's eyes grow wide. "And I like magic so much because I was a cardsharp?"

Wilcox smiles. "Perhaps. But don't read too much into this. Learning from your experiences in *this* life is the main point. Be thankful you've created some good karma in the past."

He squeezes Jerry's arm. "You have suffered a great deal recently, and that is when Grace is apt to descend. When your ego is crushed, that is when your Higher Self can help.

"You need to help your mom now. Go home and do your best. Ask your Higher Self for guidance. And try to get some rest."

"I will. Thanks, Wilcox!"

SIXTEEN

JERRY tries to get some rest, but he loses track of time.

The nights and days rush by in a black-and-white blur. He asks his Higher Self for guidance. He prays for "the best" for his mom. He sits up late with her, even though Mrs. March is there.

After Mrs. Broonlik arrives in the morning, Jerry goes through the motions of school. But his mother keeps getting worse. It's like a strange, repeating nightmare . . .

At last, his mother agrees to see a specialist! She and Jerry travel in an ambulance. Dr. Torque is completely bald except for two shaggy white tufts just above his ears. He clears his throat a lot. He solemnly tests Jerry's mom in a zillion ways . . . and then gives up.

"I've never seen anything like this," he declares.

Jerry's heart sinks like a stone in a dark, murky lake.

At night, Jerry prays and prays. Is there any way his Higher Self can connect with his mother's Higher Self? They're both from the same source, aren't they?

He doesn't want his mom to cheat her karma. But he keeps hoping that between praying for the best for her and praying for her to be cured, there is a little "wiggle room." He humbly dares to pray for this. And he thinks, gratefully, of how well she's always fed him and cared for him.

His mom is feverish, delirious. She moans. She's suffering so much! Should he use The Look, like he did with Eva?

The next night (or is it several nights later?), Mrs. March calls to say she's sick and can't come.

Jerry sits on a chair in his mother's shadowy room. She turns restlessly, tangled up in the blanket. She groans fitfully in her sleep. It's about two a.m.

Jerry manages to straighten the blanket without waking her. He meditates deeply, thinking of his Higher Self, praying for what is best . . .

His mom makes weak, moaning sounds, breathing with difficulty.

Jerry feels her wrist. Her pulse is barely there. Shivers of fright prickle down his spine. He senses that the end might be near.

Sitting on the chair, he prays desperately. *Just a little wiggle room for her to get well. Please!*

He's exhausted. After a while, his eyes slowly grow blurry . . .

Jerry enters a state of intense reverie, almost like a dream. He sees differently now. A luminous haze floats high above his mother.

The haze seems to gather itself, pulling together. Jerry gasps. Is that his father's shining face? Yes! It's his father, and he's smiling down at them.

"Dad!" Jerry whispers. "Dad!" A flood of childhood memories fills his head. His papa reads him *Howard the Happy Basset Hound,* hugs him tight, kisses his cheek . . .

For some mysterious reason, Jerry remembers how he himself floated near the ceiling, outside his body, when he was very young. Could anyone have seen him then? How can he see his father now? *Your minds are connected.* Is his love for his father bringing them together, like Wilcox said? Is that why he can see his father's face?

Suddenly the face is Eva's. Her hollow, sunken eyes are peaceful. Her smile is beautiful and calm.

Now Eva is Peter. "We'll all be dead before the year is over," he says, grinding his teeth.

Peter spreads out his charms on the little blue bag. He touches the green glass cat and the wooden basset hound. Jerry's eyes grow wide. *Jade and Lowey!* "It's all part of Nature's Grand Design," says Wilcox's voice. "It's all part of our waking dream."

"A cat has nine lives," his mother's voice declares. She laughs sadly.

The head of a grinning cat floats on the blackboard. "A secret between good friends," says Mr. Stim. "Remember our little secret," says the thin lady with bright-red hair. "Let sleeping dogs lie," says Dr. Kurr.

Wilcox laughs and laughs. "You were using part of The Look," he says.

Lowey hisses like a teakettle.

"Aw," says Suzie. "He's so cute!"

Mrs. Broomstick cackles. It echoes crazily in Jerry's head, like the eerie laughter in a funhouse.

He sees his father's smiling face again. "What time is it when the clock strikes thirteen, Jerry? I'm outside of time now. Everything is *now*." His father's face moves down closer.

Then it hits Jerry hard, *really* hard. He freezes in terror. His father has come to take his mother away! He wants her to join him, go with him. Jerry opens his mouth, but nothing comes out. His lips are trembling. They might shatter like ice if he could talk.

His father seems to understand. Something like a hand points to his eyes. *I'm only watching over you.*

"Dad!" Jerry cries. "Dad!"

His mother groans, opens her eyes. "Jerry. I was having a dream. Making mushroom soup, and . . ." She turns her head. "What's wrong? What are you staring at?"

She doesn't see his father at all! How can that be?

"I . . . I don't know, Mom." He squeezes her hand. Should he tell her if she can't see him? He glances up again, bewildered.

His father's smiling face shimmers away.

Jerry takes three deep breaths. "I thought I saw a light, but . . ."

"Jerry, could you please get me some more water?"

"Yeah, sure, Mom."

She raises herself on one elbow. "What happened?" Her voice is strong. "I feel so much better!"

"You do? That's great!" He snatches up her empty glass.

Looking back as he runs for the water, Jerry collides with the doorjamb. His shoulder is probably bruised, but he doesn't even notice it. He feels a warm inner glow.

SEVENTEEN

WILCOX! Are you there?

Yes, Jerry. How's it going?

Good news! My mom is much better.

That's wonderful!

Dr. Trainer says it's a medical miracle. He can't account for it at all.

But maybe we can. Were you praying the way I suggested?

Yes. And I think it helped. But I couldn't keep from praying for a little wiggle room.

What?

Wiggle room. Between praying for the best . . . and praying for her to be cured.

Interesting. It sounds like you were praying for Grace. And your praying may have been answered. I think you have achieved a good deal of mastery. But you sound tired. Your thoughts are coming through faintly. Please get some rest, and then come to see me.

I will. Thanks, Wilcox. I've got a lot to tell you!

Acknowledgments

Special thanks to Paul Cash for his vital insights. I'm also grateful to Jeff Cox and my wife Eleanor. And to Paul Brunton for the "Yoga of the Liberating Smile" and to P.G. Wodehouse for "The Smile That Wins." Of course, they bear no responsibility for any mistakes that Jerry or I may have made.

Also in this series

Jerry's Magic (2014)

Jerry's Madness (2015)

Jerry's Mystery (2016)